THREE LITTLE PIGS

Retold by Heather Amery
Illustrated by Stephen Cartwright

Language consultant: Betty Root
Series editor: Jenny Tyler

There's a little yellow duck to find on every page.

A Mother Pig has three baby pigs.

One day she says, "You've grown too big for my little house. It's time you had houses of your own."

The three little Pigs trot down the road.

"Goodbye," calls Mother Pig. "Build your houses and never open the door to the Big Bad Wolf. He'll eat you."

The first little Pig meets a man.

He has a big bundle of straw. "Please give me some straw,"
says the little Pig. The man gives him lots of straw.

The little Pig builds his house.

He is very proud of it. It has two doors, two windows and
a fine roof. "I'll be safe and snug inside," he says.

The second little Pig meets a man.

He has a big load of sticks. "Please give me some sticks,"
says the little Pig. The man gives him lots of big sticks.

The little Pig builds his house.

It has strong walls, two doors, two windows and a chimney.

"I'll be safe and snug inside," he says.

The third little Pig meets a man.

He has a load of bricks. "Please give me some bricks," says the little Pig. The man gives him all he needs for his house.

The little Pig builds his house.

It has thick walls, two doors, two windows and a chimney.

"I'm not afraid of the Big Bad Wolf," he says.

The Wolf comes to the straw house.

"Little Pig, let me in," he says. "No, Mr. Wolf," says the
Pig. The Wolf huffs and puffs, and blows the house down.

The little Pig runs to the stick house.

Soon the Wolf comes to the door. "Little Pigs, let me in," he says. "No, no, we won't, Mr. Wolf," say the two little Pigs.

The Wolf huffs and puffs, and blows the house down.

The two little Pigs run to the brick house. Soon the Wolf comes to the door. "Little Pigs, let me in," he says.

"No, no, no, we won't," say the Pigs.

The Wolf huffs and puffs. He puffs and huffs but he can't blow the house down. He looks around for a way in.

The Wolf jumps onto the roof.

He looks down the chimney. The three little Pigs put a big pot of water on the stove. "We're ready now," says one.

The Wolf slides down the chimney.

He falls into the big pot of water. One little Pig puts on
the lid. "That's the end of the Big Bad Wolf," he says.

"Now we'll have supper."

"You can stay in my house," says one little Pig, "and the Big
Bad Wolf can never, ever frighten us again."

This edition first published in 2003 by Usborne Publishing Ltd, 83-85 Saffron Hill, London EC1N 8RT, England. www.usborne.com
Copyright © 2003, 1996 Usborne Publishing Ltd.
The name Usborne and the devices 🔅 🌐 are Trade Marks of Usborne Publishing Ltd. All rights reserved. No part of this publication may be reproduced,
stored in a retrieval system, or transmitted in any form or by any means, electronic, mechanical, photocopying, recording
or otherwise, without prior permission of the publisher. UE. This edition first published in America in 2003. Printed in China.